Happy Cat

For my parents, who always let me draw

I LIKE TO READ is a registered trademark of Holiday House, Inc.

Copyright © 2013 by Steve Henry
All Rights Reserved
HOLIDAY HOUSE is registered in the U.S. Patent and Trademark Office.
Printed and Bound in April 2014 at Tien Wah Press, Johur Bahru, Johor, Malaysia.
The text typeface is Report School.
The artwork was created with watercolor, gouache, ink, and brown craft paper
on Arches Hot Pressed Watercolor Paper.
www.holidayhouse.com
3 5 7 9 10 8 6 4 2

Library of Congress Cataloging-in-Publication Data
Henry, Steve.
Happy Cat / Steve Henry. — 1st ed.
p. cm. — (I like to read)
ISBN 978-0-8234-2659-1 (hardcover)
[1. Cats—Fiction. 2. Animals—Fiction. 3. Apartment houses—Fiction.] I. Title.
PZ7.H39732Hap 2013
[E]—dc23
2012006579

ISBN 978-0-8234-3177-9 (paperback)

Happy Cat

by **Steve Henry**

Holiday House / New York

Cat was cold.

He went in.

Cat met Rat.

Cat went up.

And Cat went up.

Cat met Dog.

Cat met Rabbit.

Cat went up.

Cat met Bird.

Cat met Elephant.

Cat went up.

He went to the top.

Cat was happy.

All were happy.

I Like to Read® Books
You will like all of them!

Visit holidayhouse.com to read more
about I Like to Read® Books.

I Like to Read® Books in Paperback
You will like all of them!

Visit http://www.holidayhouse.com/I-Like-to-Read/ for
more about I Like to Read® books, including flash cards,
reproducibles, and the complete list of titles.